VROOOM,

BEACH LANE BOOKS NEW YORK • LONDON • TORONTO • SYDNEY • NEW DELHI

VROOOM!

● **Mary Lyn Ray** ● **Julien Chung**

This is how I drive my car.

I hold the wheel.

I turn the key. And . . .

To other cars I say:

HONK! HO

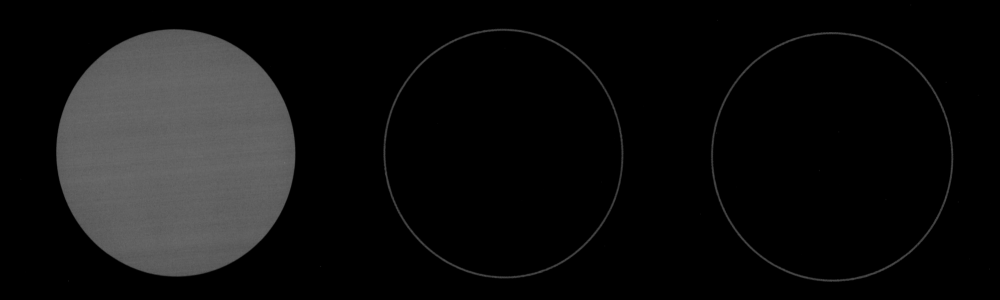

Every driver must know the rules: stop when the light is red,

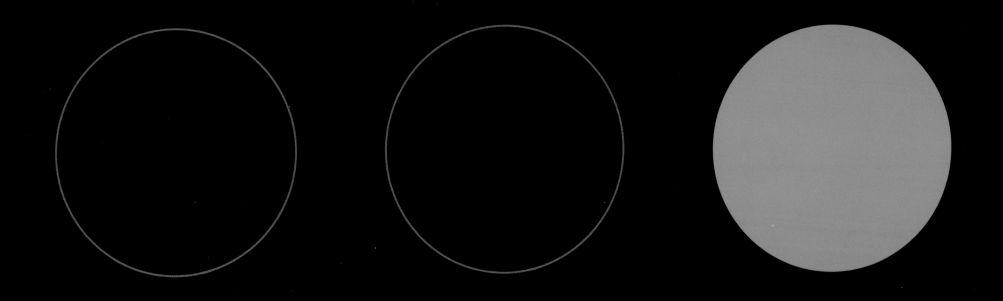

go when the light is green.

Follow the yellow line:
around, around—

and up

and down

and under.

Pay the toll at the toll booth.

If something is broken,
go to the Fix-It Garage.

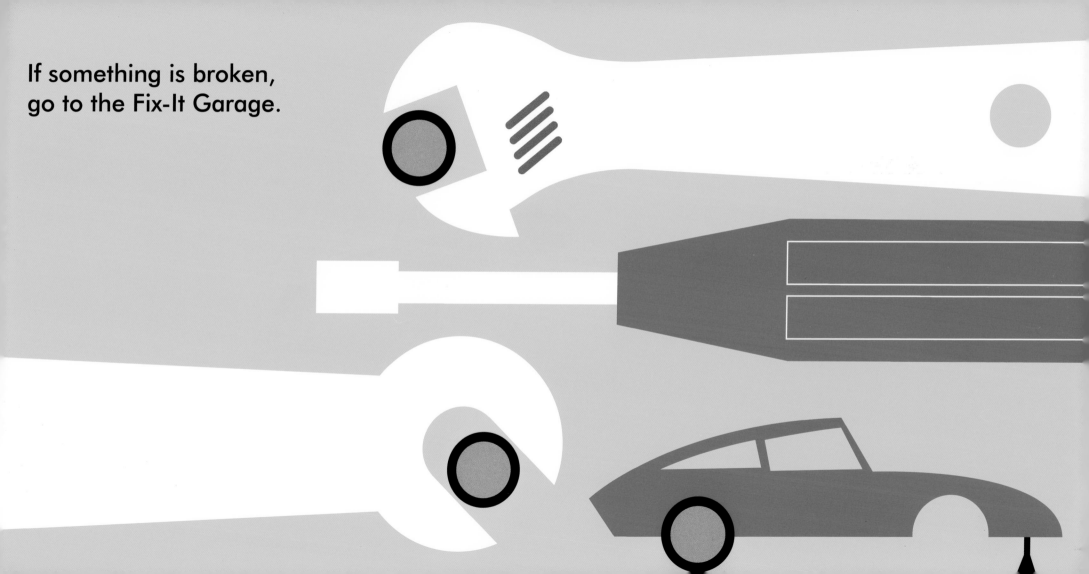

Now here's the way to Far Away—

DRIVE,

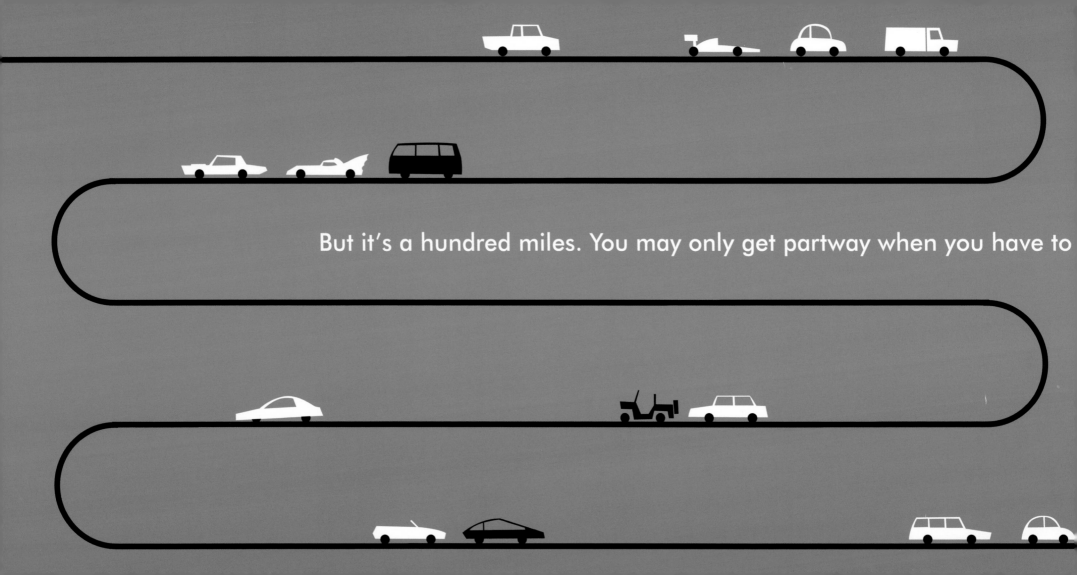

But it's a hundred miles. You may only get partway when you have to go home for lunch.

Lunch is all-the-letters soup.

I save C, A, R for last.

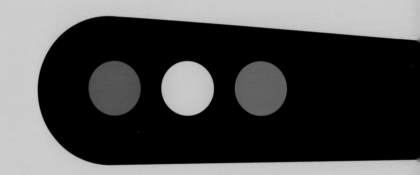

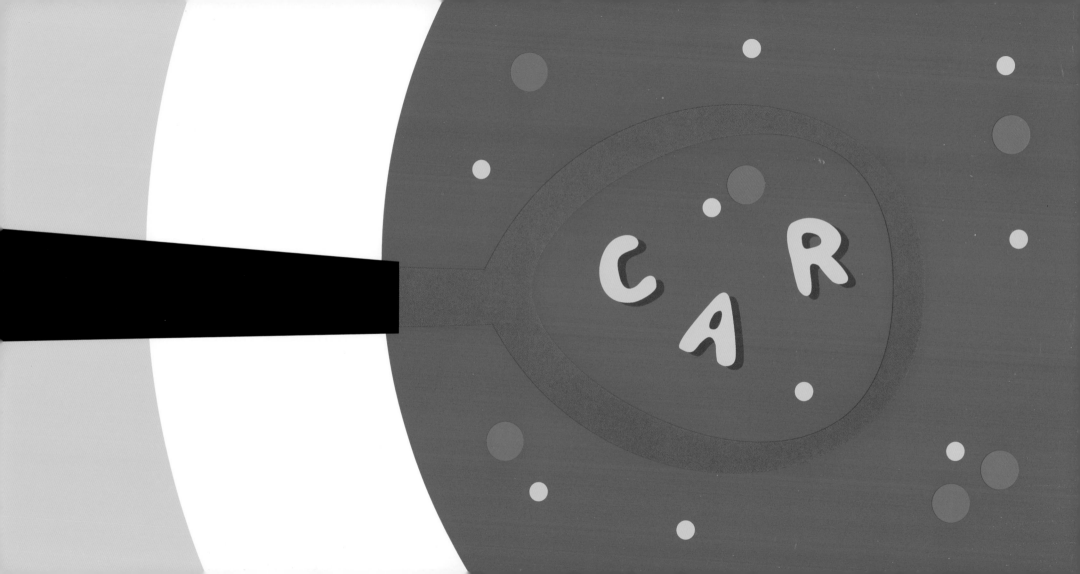

After it drives fast,
my car is tired.

So it has a little nap.

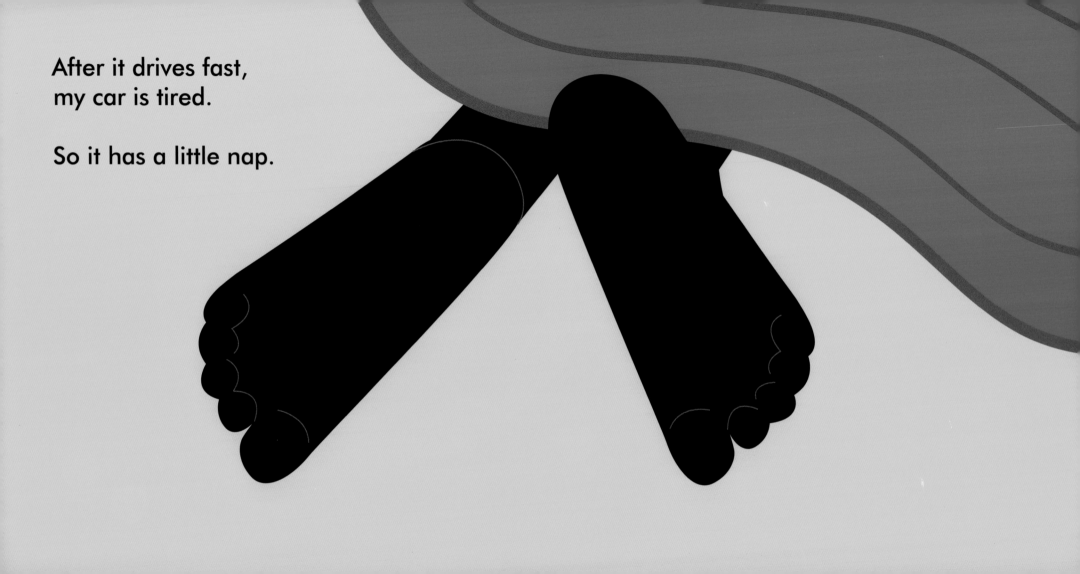

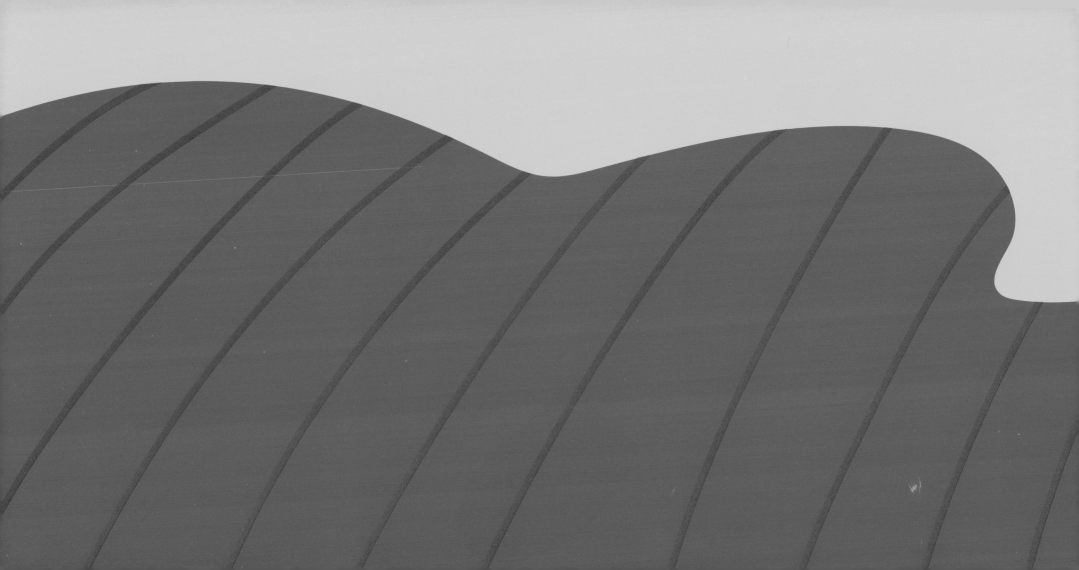

Then wake up! Start up!

And when the light turns green—

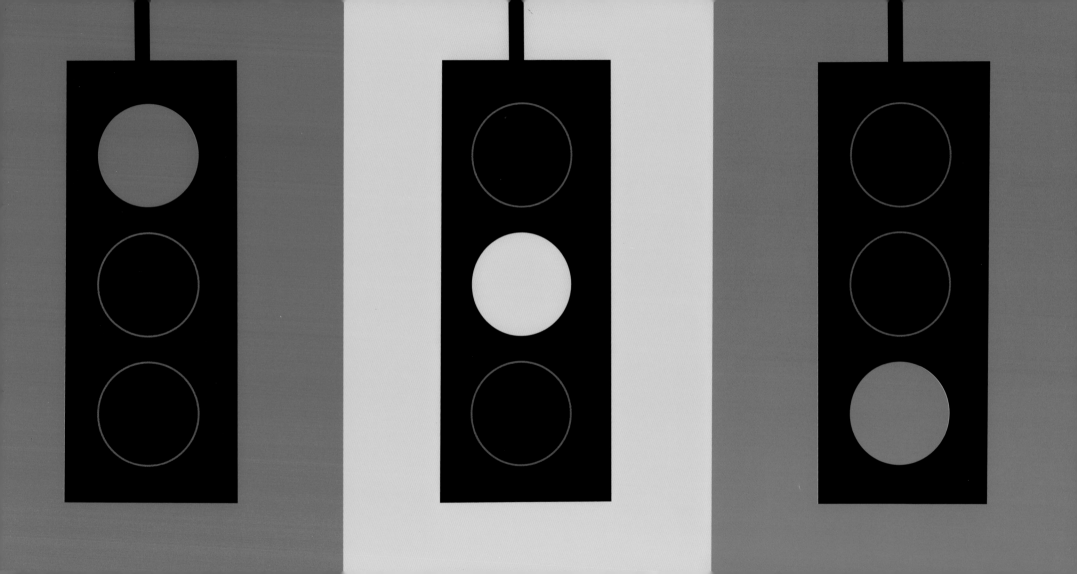

G is G. O is O.

For a small boy with a small car
that he drove a very long way
—M. L. R.

BEACH LANE BOOKS • An imprint of Simon
& Schuster Children's Publishing Division • 1230
Avenue of the Americas, New York, New York 10020 • Text
© 2021 by Mary Lyn Ray • Illustration © 2021 by Julien Chung •
Book design © 2021 by Simon & Schuster, Inc. • All rights reserved,
including the right of reproduction in whole or in part in any form. • BEACH
LANE BOOKS and colophon are trademarks of Simon & Schuster, Inc. • For
information about special discounts for bulk purchases, please contact Simon &
Schuster Special Sales at 1-866-506-1949 or business@simonandschuster.com. •